Jenny and the Thunder-Kicker

By Alessandro Reale

Cover art by Senyphine

Copyright © 2019 by Alessandro Reale

ISBN-13: 978-1795322270

You can't always wait for the storm to pass. You have to face it.

That's how you deal with anything that scares you.

To Jake

Chapter 1

Little Jenny Spotter was terrified of thunder. After all, what little boy or girl wouldn't be? It was loud, it made her house shake, and it always came after super bright flashes of lightning. Jenny was amazed that nobody else in her house was afraid of the thunder. Not her mom, not her dad, not even her baby brother, Danny! A clap of thunder could strike right over the Spotter house at any minute, and everyone would go about their day. Mom would keep working in her office, Dad would keep watching TV, and Danny would keep sleeping (like all babies do). The Spotters would live their normal lives.

Except for Jenny.

Any time it started raining, Jenny would run right into her mom's office, curl up under her desk, and try her hardest to cover her ears from that loud BOOM!

"The thunder can't hurt you, dear," her mom would tell her.

But Jenny knew better.

"If it can't hurt me, then why's it so loud?"

Her mom would then roll her eyes and repeat herself. "It can't hurt you."

Jenny knew her mom couldn't understand. So when it started raining pretty hard one Saturday night, she went to her dad, hoping he would help her.

"The thunder can't hurt you, Jenny," said her dad as she crawled onto his lap.

At that moment, the first clap of thunder struck overhead. Jenny squealed and buried her face into her dad's shoulder. Dad rubbed her back until the rumbling stopped. When Jenny looked up, she saw that he was giggling!

"That's not funny! It's so loud!" She looked up at the ceiling, expecting another boom at any second. "Why is it so loud?"

Her dad didn't roll his eyes like her mom did. Instead, he smiled.

"Because of the Thunder-Kickers."

"What are Thunder-Kickers?" she asked, trying to distract herself.

"They're giants that live up in the sky," her dad explained. "They kick clouds so hard that they cause thunder."

Jenny was confused. She once heard a boy in her class say that his parents told him that thunder was caused by giants bowling. But then their teacher said it wasn't true. Now Dad is saying that there are giants kicking clouds up there. Was somebody lying?

"Why do they kick the clouds?" asked Jenny.

"It's their job. Whenever lightning hits, they kick the cloud to let us know how far away the storm is."

Jenny stared out the window. This time, she saw the bright flash light up the sky. Then, a few seconds later, thunder gently rumbled nearby. Jenny whimpered, ready to hide in Dad's arms again, but he smiled and pointed.

"See? The less time between the lightning and the thunder, the closer the storm is. And if the thunder is quiet, it means the storm is almost done. This storm won't be around for long, and the Thunder-Kickers will be on their way."

"I hope it's done soon," said Jenny. "The thunder scares me."

"Just because something sounds scary doesn't mean it can hurt you."

"But can't the Thunder-Kickers hurt us?" reasoned Jenny.

Dad rolled his eyes but didn't answer the question. He patted Jenny's head and let her sit with him until the storm passed.

Learning about the Thunder-Kickers made Jenny feel a little better. Now that she knew where thunder came from, she didn't think it was as scary. But she wasn't too happy knowing there were giants living in the sky, causing so much noise and scaring little kids like her. Who do they think they are?

Jenny didn't need to hide under her mom's desk or on her dad's lap anymore when it rained. Now she would hide under her blanket, holding her plastic sword and peeking out the window.

Once the rain started, she'd look up and say, "You better keep it down up there!" while waving her sword. However, the moment thunder struck, she'd bury her face in her pillow and cover her head with the blanket.

The Thunder-Kickers either didn't hear Jenny's warnings, or they just didn't care, because they kept doing their job. At least once a week, there would be another storm over the town of Hazel Grove. Sometimes there would be two storms in the same day! It was a rainy April, so those Thunder-Kickers must've been really busy. Jenny kept her sword close by; those Thunder-Kickers would be sorry if they didn't stop scaring her.

Then, one day, the rain stopped, and it was sunny for a whole month straight. Jenny was as happy as could be.

Did the Thunder-Kickers finally hear her warnings? Were they fired from their jobs?

The summer came along, and the sun kept shining. Jenny laughed and played without a care in the world. It seemed like the Thunder-Kickers would never come around Hazel Grove ever again. That is, until one day, when Jenny overheard her parents talking.

"I'm running out to get groceries before the rain."

"There's rain coming?"

"Weather channel says a storm's on its way."

The Thunder-Kickers were coming back! Jenny could already feel her knees shaking. Why was the weather channel telling them to come back? Don't they know they don't belong here? She now understood why her Dad would often say mean things about that guy on TV who always brought the bad weather.

Jenny was a little scared, but also a little angry. She marched up to her room, grabbed her sword from the back of the closet, and took her spot under her trusted blanket. From where she was sitting, she could see dark clouds rolling over her neighborhood. They were darker than any she'd ever seen before in her life. Looks like there was a bunch of Thunder-Kickers coming this time.

But the thunder didn't come. It rained for a long time, and there was even a flash or two of lightning, but Jenny didn't hear a single rumble or clap of thunder after.

It rained for what felt like forever. Soon, Jenny felt her eyelids getting heavy, but she fought to keep them open. She wanted to stay up in case the Thunder-Kickers started making noise. Her sword was lying by her side, ready for a fight.

Jenny fell asleep to the sound of the pouring rain.

Chapter 2

Jenny woke up to a strange crash. It was unlike anything she'd ever heard before in her life. When she peeked out the window, she saw it was still raining. Was it thunder that caused that noise?

No, it didn't sound like any thunderclap she'd ever heard. It sounded… different.

There was a blinding flash of lightning. Jenny threw her blanket over her head, waiting for the scary boom that was bound to follow. But after a few minutes, she noticed it wasn't coming. Where was the thunder?

Jenny was about to go back to bed, both relieved yet still scared, when she thought she saw something out of the corner of her eye in the backyard. It was nighttime, so she couldn't make out much, but she was certain that there was something moving back there. It might've been the neighbor's cat, Bumpy, coming to use Mom's garden as a bathroom again.

No, this wasn't Bumpy. Or any cat.

It was much bigger.

Jenny didn't have to think twice. She ran into her parents' bedroom (bringing her sword with her) and pounced on their bed.

"Mom! Dad! There's something in the backyard! I think it's a monster!"

If Jenny's yells didn't wake up her parents, the plastic sword smacking them in the face did.

"Ow!" said her dad. "Put that away before you take an eye out. Why are you awake?"

"I told you, Dad! There's a monster in the backyard. I just saw it! I thought it was Mr. Gerstein's cat pooping in the garden again but this thing was bigger than Bumpy and had a billion arms and—"

There was a cry from the corner of the room.

Uh-oh, Jenny thought. She had accidentally woken up Danny. Her baby brother's crying sounded like a fire truck, and it was almost as loud as the thunderclap she heard earlier. Mom jumped out of bed and went to pick him up while Dad sat up and rubbed his eyes.

"Jenny, what are you talking about?"

"Dad, I promise there's a monster in our yard. Please, come look out my window!"

Mom was humming a tune while she rocked back and forth with Danny in her arms. "Just go take a look, David. Maybe there *is* a monster out there."

Jenny thought she saw a small smile on her parents' faces. How could they be smiling when there was a thunderstorm going on and a monster in the backyard?!

"Come on, Dad. Before it gets away!"

Without another word, Jenny's dad stood up, grabbed her by the hand, and followed her back to her room.

"Look! Right out there, in the corner of the yard." Jenny happily pointed out the window. Dad rubbed his eyes and followed her gaze.

There was a moment of silence (aside from the pouring rain). Finally, Dad spoke.

"I don't see any monster."

Jenny didn't want to admit it, but she didn't see anything either. The giant dark thing she saw a few minutes ago had disappeared. Did the monster escape? She raised her toy sword protectively to her chest.

"Honey, please put that down."

"Dad, I saw a monster, and now he's gone! What if he gets into the house? Did we lock all the doors? Do you and Mom need weapons? I've got my field hockey stick under my bed..."

"We're fine, Jenny. The doors are locked. Nobody will get into this house, especially a monster."

"But what if they do get in?"

"Then I'll kick them back out!"

"But what if the monster eats you?"

Dad smiled. "Then he'll have to deal with your mother, and then he'll be sorry!"

He kissed Jenny on the cheek and returned to his room. Jenny wasn't happy with his answer. She was already worried about the thunder; now she had to worry about a monster sneaking around her yard. Jenny looked at her sword, thinking that it might not be enough to protect her family.

The lightning flashed again. Jenny didn't bother counting this time. Whatever was going on, it looked like there wasn't going to be any thunder during this storm, which was probably a good thing. But Jenny had noticed something odd when the lightning flashed. For that split-second, when her backyard was lit up, she saw a weird shape in the far corner, behind her pool. It was a big, light blue thing, like a giant blanket. Maybe the pool cover had blown off again?

Or maybe, it was something else.

Jenny was about to go get her dad again, but she knew it wasn't a good idea. He would think she was lying again. It'd be like the time she told her parents that her teacher didn't give her any homework and that she could watch TV all night. Now, Jenny *had* been lying back then, but her parents knew right away that she wasn't telling the truth. And after what happened a few minutes ago, she knew she had no chance of convincing them.

No, Jenny would have to do this all by herself.

Grabbing her raincoat, her rain boots, and, of course, her trusty sword, Jenny made her way downstairs and to the backdoor.

The rain was still pounding heavily, as it had been for the past couple of hours. At least there wasn't any lightning or thunder…

The clock on the microwave said 12:35. Jenny had never been up this late, except for last year when she had a bad tummy ache and kept barfing all night. But her parents didn't care if she was up late then. If they found out she was awake *and* going outside at this hour, she'd probably be grounded for the rest of her life.

Standing on her tippy-toes, Jenny managed to barely reach the lock to the backdoor. She was careful to slide it open as quietly as possible. With her sword in hand, she slowly walked outside into the pouring rain.

Even though it was raining hard, it wasn't that loud. It only sounded loud inside because it was pounding on the side of the house. Out here, it was pretty quiet. Just the constant sound of *click, click, click* as the rain hit the grass.

It was dark outside, but Jenny could make out most of the backyard, thanks to the big moon poking through the storm clouds. One of the lawn chairs had blown onto its side, and there was a bunch of water filling up the uncovered fire-pit. The pool sat by the fence with its cover still on. Next to the pool was the tall tree that Jenny and her friends played under. Most of the branches had fallen off and were scattered all over the yard.

Jenny felt her heart skip a beat when she glimpsed a light blue behind the pool in the corner of the yard.

Her sword was ready.

The rain wasn't falling as hard now. The storm must've finally been moving on. Still, Jenny was carefully listening for the sudden crack of thunder to come out of nowhere (despite the fact that she hadn't heard a single one all night).

She walked toward the pool. The light blue thing fluttered in the wind. What was it, and was it covering something? Jenny knew she should've gone to get her parents, but her curiosity got the best of her. She was going to find out exactly what was behind the blue thing, and if it was going to cause any trouble, then it better be ready to deal with the business end of her sword.

As Jenny crept around the pool, the blue thing shook. Maybe Bumpy was under it. Or maybe it was a stray dog. Jenny always wanted a dog, but she knew her parents would never let her have one, especially one she found hiding in her backyard after a storm.

Jenny moved closer. Now she was a few feet away, and she could see that the blue thing was a giant blanket that her dad would use to cover up the barbecue during the winter. He called it a, "tarp," which Jenny always thought was a funny word. The tarp stopped moving when Jenny got close. She took a deep breath and grabbed the bottom of the tarp. She whispered *Three... Two... One...*, and then yanked it away.

Chapter 3

"MOM! DAD!"

Jenny ran inside so fast that she didn't even bother taking off her rain gear or closing the backdoor. Instead, she bolted straight up to her parents' room and jumped on the bed, still soaked and still holding onto her sword.

Dad sat up first. "What?! What's going on? Why are you soaking wet?"

Mom yelled and rolled out of bed as the sheets became drenched. Jenny could hardly breathe because she was so excited and scared. She didn't think to apologize for getting the sheets wet, or for waking Danny up again. Her little brother's cries were louder than the rain, which had gone back to its heavy downpour.

"Dad, I went into the backyard and I saw something behind the pool, and when I went t—"

"Wait a minute, wait a minute, wait a minute," Dad said quickly, rubbing his eyes. "You went outside, in this weather, at this time of night?"

"Yeah, but only—"

"Jenny, you *never* leave this house at nighttime without me or your mother, especially if there's a thunderstorm outside. Do you understand?"

"I didn't me—"

"Do you understand?" Dad repeated.

"Please, listen to me!" Jenny pleaded, slapping her fist down on the sheets. "I went outside because I saw something weird behind the pool. And when I went to check, there was a giant man hiding under a tarp!"

Dad quickly looked at Mom, who had stopped rocking Danny back and forth. Slowly, Dad said, "You saw a man in our backyard?"

When Jenny nodded excitedly, her dad said a word she had heard once in a movie but was told to never ever repeat. She knew her dad wasn't happy.

"Call the police," Dad told Mom. Turning to Jenny, he said, "Stay here with your mother and brother. Do not leave this room, no matter what."

Jenny wanted to say something, but nodded again to show she understood. Dad threw on his jacket and pants and went downstairs. Meanwhile, Mom balanced Danny in her arm while using her free hand to dial her cell phone. Jenny sat on the edge of the bed in silence.

"Hello, my name is Irene Spotter and I live at 510 Monroe Avenue... yes, in Hazel Grove. My daughter said she saw a man hiding in our backyard."

"A *giant* man, Mom!" piped up Jenny. "Tell them it was a *giant* man."

"Shush, honey. Sorry, a *giant* man... No, me and my husband were asleep and she woke us up to tell us. She said she went outside and found him hiding in the yard... We're all in the bedroom, but my husband went to check... Okay, thank you so much... Yes, I can stay on the line..."

Dad returned seconds later. He was holding a broom handle in one hand and a flashlight in the other.

"They said there's a patrol car around the corner," said Mom, cradling the phone on her shoulder while gently rocking Danny. He had been asleep for a while, but Mom refused to put him down.

"Good," said Dad, taking a seat next to Jenny. "I closed and locked the backdoor."

"You mean it was still open?!" Mom asked, her eyes bugging out.

Jenny looked at her feet. "Um, I might've forgot to close it."

Dad rubbed his daughter's head. "It's okay. You were scared. I didn't see anything inside besides some of the mud that Jenny tracked in, so I think we're fine. And I didn't see anything around the pool either."

"Not even the tarp?"

"No, not even the tarp. So either the giant man is gone, or he's hiding. The police will find him, though."

Jenny's lip quivered. She was scared, but she was also sorry for causing all this trouble. She hugged her dad and started to cry.

"I'm sorry, Dad. I didn't mean to scare you. I saw something outside and went to look. I didn't know it would be this bad."

Dad kissed her on the head. Mom sat on the opposite side of Jenny and kissed her as well.

"Everything's okay, honey," said Dad. "The police will be here soon. Just promise me and your mom that you won't ever go outside in the dark alone again."

"I promise," Jenny said almost instantly.

And she meant it. Jenny would never go outside at night again, especially during a thunderstorm.

By the time the police came, Jenny had already gone to bed; she was spending the night in Mom and Dad's room. Mom stayed with her while Dad talked to the policewoman in the kitchen. Jenny had her eyes closed and pretended to be asleep, but she could hear everything the grown-ups were talking about. The officer said it was probably a homeless man who was trying to stay out of the rain. She told Dad that there wasn't anything to worry about, but the police were looking around the house to see if they could find anything.

About an hour later, Jenny still hadn't fallen asleep. Another officer came inside and said they couldn't find anything in the backyard. No footprints, no tarp, no anything. Dad said he didn't see anything either but wanted to be completely sure. One of the officers asked him if he thought Jenny just had a nightmare and got scared (if Jenny wasn't pretending to be asleep, she would've gone out and said that it definitely wasn't a nightmare!).

Dad's laugh echoed down the hallway. "I think this is partially my fault. I told Jenny the Thunder-Kicker story and her imagination must've gotten carried away."

Now the policewoman laughed. "Oh, jeez. You told her the story about the Thunder-Kickers? My dad told me that one when I was a kid. It's a classic."

"Yeah, but it looks like Jenny might've taken it a bit too seriously. You should've seen what happened when we first told her about the Easter Bunny..."

Jenny grumbled (knowing no one would hear her). Her parents always brought up the time she set a booby trap for the Easter Bunny and the next morning she had to clean up a smashed carton of eggs from the dining room floor. It was one time!

After a few more minutes of talking, Dad thanked the police officers and told them to stay dry as they left. The rain hadn't stopped at all.

Dad came into the bedroom. Mom was sitting in the chair next to Danny's crib. Jenny kept her eyes closed.

"I think we're fine," whispered Dad. "The police thought it was probably a homeless guy trying to find a dry place to sleep. But they didn't find anything around the house."

"I heard," replied Mom. "Do you think Jenny's imagination was running wild again? You know how she gets during these storms…"

"I wish I could say for sure if it was her imagination, but I'd rather be safe than sorry."

Jenny couldn't take it anymore. She sat up.

"It wasn't my imagination! I saw a giant man hiding under a tarp in our backyard!"

"Shhh," said Dad. "We believe you, Jenny. But this is a very scary situation. We want to be sure you're okay."

Jenny didn't say another word. She knew what she saw, no matter what her parents said.

"Let's get you to bed," said Dad. He took Jenny's hand and led her down the hallway. When they got back to her room, she slowly climbed into bed. Dad kissed her on the forehead.

"This was a big night for you, dear. Now it's time for you to go to sleep."

Jenny looked out the window.

"Dad, why hasn't there been any thunder tonight?"

"What do you mean?"

"I saw a lot of lightning and rain, but I didn't hear any thunder all night. What happened?"

Dad glanced out the window.

"Honestly, I don't know."

"Do you think the Thunder-Kickers aren't doing their job?" asked Jenny.

"Maybe," said Dad, shrugging. "Or maybe they've gone to bed, like you should."

Dad left the room and closed the door behind him, leaving Jenny alone in the dark. Her window blinds were closed, preventing her from seeing her backyard. She was tempted to go check if the blue tarp was still near the pool, even if the police said they didn't see it.

But what if it was? Would she tell her parents again? Then the police would have to come and look around again, and the tarp would be gone. Maybe it *was* her imagination...

Jenny pulled the covers up to her chin and rolled over. She knew what she saw. It was a giant man hiding in her backyard. And when she pulled the tarp away, she looked into his eyes, and she knew he wouldn't hurt her. In fact, he looked scared, like a lost puppy.

The ceiling over Jenny's bed creaked loudly. The house made funny noises from time to time. It didn't bother Jenny, which was odd since she was terrified of the sound of thunder. Her dad explained how houses, especially old ones, always creak when there's a lot of wind or rain.

This creaking was different, though. There'd be a creak, a pause, then another creak, then another pause, then two or three creaks. And it sounded like they were crossing from one side of the ceiling to the other. Back and forth. It almost sounded like a man walking across the roof.

A giant man.

Jenny sat up. Her heart was bouncing around in her chest. Her eyes followed the creaking back and forth across the ceiling.

Creak, creak.

Silence.

Creak, creak, creak, creak.

Jenny leaped out of bed and went for the door, but stopped right before she grabbed the knob. This time, she wasn't going to tell her parents about what might be her imagination again. She had heard the story about the boy who cried wolf. He kept telling people a wolf was coming, and the people believed him, but it turned out he was lying. Then, when the wolf finally *did* come, nobody believed the boy. Jenny wasn't going to cry wolf.

But what if the wolf was actually here now?

Her trusty sword was in her hand once again (Jenny had to beg her dad to give it back after what happened). She was smarter this time. Jenny wasn't going to go outside (not that she'd ever be able to get up on the roof). Maybe she could see from her window. All she had to do was open it up a tiny bit and look up. That wasn't breaking her promise to Dad.

Slowly, Jenny moved to her window, careful not to make too much noise. She grabbed the cords to raise her blinds. With one big tug, she yanked them open.

And she found herself face-to-face with the giant man.

Chapter 4

Jenny covered her mouth with her sleeve to hide
her scream. The giant wasn't as quick-thinking. He let out
a howl that was luckily not as loud as the pouring rain. He
stumbled backwards and appeared to trip over his feet.
Jenny braced herself for an earthquake as the giant
landed on his butt in her backyard, but it never came. He
landed as softly as if he fell onto a pile of pillows. The
giant stood up, rubbed his behind, and slowly approached

the window. Jenny saw that his fall didn't cause any damage to the yard. It was like he was as light as a cloud.

Even through the darkness, Jenny could see the giant's face clearly. He had dark, rough-looking skin, like a potato, and his thin, white, soaked hair fell to his shoulders. He wore a light blue shirt and matching blue pants, and Jenny saw that the blue tarp from earlier was wrapped around his neck, like a cape!

It took everything in Jenny's power not to scream. She was looking at a real-life a giant. This was like something out of one of her fairy tale books. The kids at school were never going to believe this!

The giant was keeping his distance. He was crouched like a scared dog, his eyes locked on the window. Jenny realized that he must've been as scared of her as she was of him (which was ridiculous because he could easily squash her with one hand). She put her toy sword down and raised both hands to show she wasn't hiding anything.

Jenny waved both her hands excitedly. The giant copied her exact movements. Then she waved only her right hand, and the giant did the same. When she did the same with her left hand, the giant waved his as well. Finally, Jenny did a little dance in front of her window. The giant stared at her and tilted his head. He then picked his nose.

"That's gross," said Jenny.

The giant stopped picking his nose and leaned forward. He reached out one of his large hands (thankfully, not the one he used to pick his nose) and poked at the window. Jenny panicked, thinking he was going to break through the glass (her sword was ready). Instead, the giant gently tapped the window twice with a *thud, thud.*

"What do you want?" Jenny whispered through the window.

The giant tilted his head. Did he hear her? Jenny was going to ask again, but the giant quickly pulled himself up onto the house with surprising speed.

Creak, creak, creak.

Jenny pressed her face up against the glass of her window to see if she could glimpse the giant now on her roof again. The edges of his feet dangled along the ledge. There was a moment of silence, and then he jumped into the air.

For a few seconds, it appeared as if he were floating like a bubble. Then he came crashing down into the yard, landing (silently) on his hands and knees. It was amazing how such a big man could make such little noise.

Jenny watched the giant brush off his knees, climb to the roof again, and then jump off, landing in the yard once more. He repeated this process at least five times before she got curious. Despite the rain still pounding away, Jenny opened her window.

"Hey!" she hissed loudly.

The giant didn't notice right away, until he tried to climb onto the roof again. Before he could lift himself up, he stopped and stared at Jenny.

"What are you doing?" she asked.

The giant said nothing. His large blue eyes studied Jenny like she was a new insect he had seen for the very first time. He smiled (revealing a mouth with missing teeth), then returned to his roof-climbing routine.

Jenny didn't know whether to keep watching him, or to tell her parents. After the fourth or fifth leap, she decided she had had enough.

"What are you doing?!" she asked again, leaning out the window. The giant didn't answer as he made his way up to the house. Jenny scowled and leaned out further. As she opened her mouth to yell, she felt her hand slip on the ledge. There was no time to react as she fell out the window.

Before Jenny even had a chance to scream, she landed on something soft yet firm. She opened her eyes and saw that the giant had caught her in his massive hand.

Now was the time for Jenny to scream. She turned and dove back into her bedroom through the open window. The giant grunted and bent over to peek in at her. Jenny reappeared with her plastic sword held high.

"Stay back, bub," she squealed. "I'm not afraid to use this!"

The giant tilted his head again. He reached one of his stubby fingers out at the window. Jenny responded by whacking it with her sword.

"I told you to stay back!" she said.

The giant yanked his finger back and frowned. Jenny thought for a second that she might've made him mad, but she didn't care. This giant was in *her* yard, and he was going to give her some answers.

"Who are you?" she asked, knowing it wouldn't do any good.

As expected, the giant paused, then put his foot on the windowsill so he could pull himself up onto the roof again. Jenny hit his big toe repeatedly with her sword, but he ignored it. His feet were like giant boulders. The sword probably felt like nothing to him.

Jenny decided it was time to try something else. Silently, she closed the window and looked around her room. Her raincoat and boots were next to the door. Her parents might've gone back to sleep by now. It was the perfect time to sneak outside, but Jenny knew that if she got caught, her parents would never let her leave the house ever again.

That meant she would have to be extra sneaky.

Jenny felt like a secret agent. The house was dark and quiet, and she was sneaking around, trying to make as little noise as possible (which was super hard since her rain boots liked to squeak and squelch). Luckily, she didn't make enough noise to wake up her parents. She'd had enough practice sneaking to the kitchen to get snacks. Still, she was extra careful with every step. She was more scared of her parents than the giant in the backyard.

Jenny softly unlocked the backdoor, scrunching her face when it made the tiniest creak. Once it was opened enough for her to fit her body, she squeezed through and went into the backyard.

The giant was still playing his roof-jump game. Now he was fluttering his arms every time he leaped. Jenny thought he looked like a huge bird learning to fly… and not doing a great job at it.

It was fun watching him do this over and over again, but Jenny didn't want to spend all night doing this. She wanted to know who he was and what he was doing in her backyard, so during one of his trips up to the roof, she made her way out into the backyard and stood right in the spot where he had landed several times. She stared at him as he prepared to launch. With a tiny grunt, he jumped high into the air, higher than any other time, and then dropped like a stone back to the ground. The giant's eyes widened as he saw the little girl beneath his feet. He spread his legs, avoiding squishing Jenny at the last second.

The giant looked down at Jenny with a befuddled frown, and Jenny stared back at him with a smile (and her sword by her side).

"Who are you?" she asked.

No answer came from the giant. At least he didn't go back to climbing the roof. This time, he got down on his knees and leaned backward, like he was listening to her tell a story.

"Fine," said Jenny. "If you won't tell me who you are, then I'll tell you about me." She sat down in the mud. "My name's Jenny Spotter, and I'm seven years old. I go to Kind Shepherd Elementary School, I'm in second grade, and I like math, peanut butter sandwiches, and baseball. I hate people who burp, braiding my hair, and that guy on TV who always talks about traffic, but only because my dad hates him." Jenny looked up the sky. "And I really, really hate thunder."

Jenny had no idea if the giant understood anything she was saying. Now she was getting really angry, but she wasn't going to give up. There must have been some way to get him to talk.

"Okay, how about this?" Jenny pointed at herself. "I'm Jenny Spotter." She held up seven fingers. "I'm seven years old." She pretended to eat an invisible sandwich. "I like peanut butter sandwiches and baseball." She swung her plastic sword like a bat.

A lightning bolt surged above them, causing the giant to look up. Jenny pointed at the sky.

"I hate thunder." She did her best to imitate the sound of thunder rumbling.

At that moment, the giant stood up and pointed at the sky as well. He then made the same rumbling sound she made, only his sounded much scarier.

"Do you hate thunder too?" asked Jenny.

The giant spotted a large rock near his foot. He pointed at the sky, then at the rock, and then kicked the rock across the yard while making his rumbling sound.

It took a few seconds for Jenny to finally understand.

"You're a Thunder-Kicker!"

Chapter 5

Jenny couldn't believe her eyes. There was a Thunder-Kicker right in her backyard! Her dad was telling the truth!

"So, why are you here?" she asked. "Why aren't you up there, kicking up thunder?"

The giant stood up quickly and turned to face the roof. Jenny ran in front of him and stretched out her arms.

"No! Not again! Tell me what you're doing here, Mr…"

There was no way the giant would tell her his name. She glanced at his blue cape.

"Tell me why you're here, Mr. Tarp."

Whether he liked his new nickname or not, Jenny would never know. But she did realize one thing after watching him jump off the roof so many times: Mr. Tarp just wanted to get home, but no matter how hard he tried, he probably wasn't going to make it.

This didn't stop Mr. Tarp, though. He stepped over Jenny and climbed the roof once more. Rather than jump off like he had been for the past hour, he began making weird hand motions and acting like he was talking to somebody. Jenny felt like she was watching a weird play.

It looked like there was someone standing beside Mr. Tarp, and he acted out both roles. First, he acted like himself, kicking the air and making rumbling sounds.

Then, he pointed at Jenny and pretended to cry while pointing at the sky and continuing the sounds.

"You're a Thunder-Kicker… and your job is to make thunder, like my dad said. But…" Mr. Tarp kept pretending to cry, this time covering his ears and making the rumbling sounds. "The thunder scared people? And you don't like scaring people?"

Mr. Tarp now acted as someone else, standing on his tip-toes (Jenny nervously moved out of the way in case he lost his balance and fell off the roof). He had his one hand on his hip and wagged his other finger up and down with a frown on his face. Mr. Tarp went back to being himself and put his hands together, as if he were begging. The (invisible) bigger giant pointed down at the ground, then kicked the air. Mr. Tarp stood at the edge of the roof and jumped off backwards, landing in the yard softly on his back.

"You were kicked out of… wherever you're from… because you didn't like to make thunder?"

Mr. Tarp frowned. Jenny now felt sorry for him. There was no way she could blame him for trying to go home, but she knew that jumping off her roof wasn't going to get him back. Her house was too small. Maybe if he was jumping from somewhere higher…

Mr. Tarp sat up and pretended to cradle a small baby in his arms. This made Jenny feel even worse.

"Do you have a baby back home?"

There was a moment where it looked like Mr. Tarp would try to climb the roof again, but he didn't. He stared at the invisible baby in his arms. Even through the rain, Jenny could see tears in his eyes.

Another lightning bolt lit up the sky. In that flash of light, Jenny caught a glimpse of Olympus Hill, the giant hill outside of town where she and her friends would ride their bikes.

Jenny had an idea.

"Don't worry, Mr. Tarp. We're going to get you home."

This wasn't going to be easy.

Normally, Jenny would never, ever leave her house or yard at night without her parents or an adult she knew, and after the stern warning her dad had given her tonight, she knew this was probably a terrible idea. But Mr. Tarp had to get home, and she was the only one who could help him.

"We're going out to the meadows, Mr. Tarp," said Jenny, pointing at Olympus Hill in the distance. The giant followed her finger, but when he saw the hill, it didn't seem to make sense to him. He looked back at the little girl and tilted his head.

"That's Olympus Hill. It's one of the tallest hills around; it's practically a mountain. You can get high enough to jump back home, I think." Jenny honestly didn't know if it would even work. At this point, she could only hope. She decided to worry about that later. Now, she wondered how she was going to make it out of town with her new friend.

There was no way Mr. Tarp would fit in the basket of her bicycle. Jenny didn't know how to drive, so her dad's truck was out of the question (Mr. Tarp was too big for that too). The best option would be to walk, but it would take forever.

"Mr. Tarp!" Jenny called out.

The giant was kicking the rock around the yard. Compared to him, it was hardly bigger than a pebble.

Even though his head hung low and he had a big frown on his face, he seemed to be having the slightest bit of fun with his new game.

"We need to get to that hill, but it's a long, long, long way. I think we have to walk."

Mr. Tarp kicked the rock again. Jenny scratched her head. Maybe if she started walking, he'd follow.

"Here, come with me!" She went over to the gate that led to the front yard and undid the latch. Looking back, she saw Mr. Tarp still kicking his rock. He was now making low rumbling noises with each kick. Jenny sighed.

This was DEFINITELY not going to be easy.

An idea popped into her head. Jenny ran to the other side of the yard and threw her hands up, signaling to Mr. Tarp to pass her the rock. It must've worked because the giant gave a toothy grin and softly kicked the rock over to her. Jenny scooped it up in her arms (it was heavier than it looked). Mr. Tarp watched her run to the front yard with his rock.

"UHHHHHHHHHHH!"

It was the loudest noise Mr. Tarp had made so far. That grunt/groan must've meant he was not happy. Jenny glanced over her shoulder as the giant stomped after her. His large steps hardly left footprints in the soaked grass and mud, and he barely made any noise (aside from that odd groaning).

Around the house Jenny ran, coming to a stop at the sidewalk. Mr. Tarp appeared in a flash. Jenny dropped the rock and pointed down the street. The empty road made the giant smile. He pulled his foot back and unleashed a kick that sent the rock hurtling down the street. Jenny cringed as the rock tumbled within feet of one of the neighbors' cars. Luckily, it made it to the end of the block without hitting anything.

Mr. Tarp slowly walked after the rock. Jenny had to run to keep up with him; for every step he took, it was like four steps for regular-sized people. It wasn't long before Jenny was out of breath.

The next kick from Mr. Tarp sent the rock even further this time. Jenny managed to sprint ahead of him, almost like she was racing him to the rock, but Mr. Tarp walked faster and beat her by a hair. His next kick was the strongest yet, and it caused the rock to go flying through the air before bouncing off a telephone pole.

"Easy!" Jenny yelled playfully.

The young girl took off down the street with her new friend close behind. Once Jenny reached the rock, she stopped to catch her breath. The rain felt great now that she had worked up a sweat, but she wasn't sure if she was going to make it all the way to Olympus Hill.

Suddenly, there was a crackling sound overhead. For a second, Jenny thought it was thunder; the first thunder-crack she heard all night. When she looked up, she saw that it was actually the telephone pole that had been hit by the rock. Mr. Tarp's kick must've been harder than they thought. The top of the pole snapped loudly, and Jenny could only watch in horror as it fell toward her. She threw her hands over her head and ducked.

Nothing happened. Jenny didn't move for a long time. As long as she kept her eyes closed, she knew nothing bad could ever happen. But her curiosity quickly got the best of her. She had to look, and when she did, she saw that Mr. Tarp was standing in front of her, holding the broken telephone pole in place.

"Wow," was all Jenny could say in shock.

Giving another toothy grin, Mr. Tarp shoved the wooden pole back into place and slowly let go. It held.

"That was so cool!" Jenny yelled.

Unfortunately, she spoke too soon. The pole started cracking again, only this time, it fell to the opposite side, and landed in the front yard of the nearby house. The cables attached to the top snapped off, sending a shower of sparks into the air.

Mr. Tarp quickly huddled over Jenny so as to protect her from the electricity crackling in the air. Jenny could see over his shoulder that the few lights that were on in the houses along the street had gone out.

"Uh, I think something bad just happened, Mr. Tarp."

The giant may not have understood what Jenny was saying, but he did look around with a worried look on his face. Without waiting one more second, he picked Jenny up in his arms and dashed down the street, kicking his stone ahead of him.

Chapter 6

Once they were far enough away, Mr. Tarp put his rock down, but he kept Jenny in his arms. She didn't mind. It definitely beat walking. And it was cool to see everything from the giant's point of view.

Mr. Tarp kicked the rock.

It went down a block and stopped next to a mailbox.

He kicked it again.

It rolled over a curb and landed on someone's lawn.

Mr. Tarp snuck onto the grass as quietly as a giant could and kicked the rock.

It didn't go as far this time. The giant had to give it another little nudge to make it go over a small hill.

Jenny started to get bored, which she thought was ridiculous because who could ever get bored with a giant? At least Mr. Tarp was being careful now. Hopefully they wouldn't have to worry about anymore accidents.

After what felt like forever, Jenny decided it was time to start walking again. She climbed down from Mr. Tarp's arms and moved to the side of the street so she could watch him kick the rock over and over without having to fear for her safety.

The rain picked up. There were small rivers forming on the sides of the street, and Jenny was keeping herself entertained in between Mr. Tarp's kicks by jumping into the water and creating huge splashes. At one point, the giant wanted to join in on the fun and stomped right behind Jenny, drenching her with a giant splash.

"Not funny!" she said to him, wagging her finger.

Mr. Tarp smiled and resumed his kicking. The rock continued rolling down the street. Jenny began skipping to keep up to the giant and his plaything. It was an odd game, but Mr. Tarp seemed to love it, and Jenny was just happy that they were finally making their way out of town.

Just then, a lightning bolt soared above their heads. Up until now, they had been ignoring the lightning because it was quiet. But this one was different. After a few seconds, there was an enormous crash that sounded like a building had fallen over. Jenny froze.

Thunder.

She could hardly move at all. The sound was so loud that it felt like her heart had stopped. Mr. Tarp seemed to have been distracted by the thunder too, and he gazed at the sky curiously. He was about to kick his rock again when he noticed Jenny wasn't rushing to his side. He looked back and saw the little girl standing completely still, petrified.

For some reason, Jenny thought that if she moved a single muscle, the thunder would strike again. She slowly moved her eyes up to the sky, waiting for the next lightning bolt to appear, which meant thunder would soon follow.

Mr. Tarp walked back up the street, bent down, and stared at her with his head slightly tilted. Jenny didn't care about their journey anymore. All she could think about was getting home and hiding under the covers until the storm was over and the thunder was gone.

When it seemed that there was no lightning coming, Jenny relaxed slightly and gained her voice. She spoke very quietly, as if her own words could cause the next clap of thunder to hit.

"I… I have to go home, Mr. Tarp."

The giant showed no reaction at first. He merely stared at the frozen girl.

Without taking her eyes off him, Jenny backed up slowly. Mr. Tarp watched her get halfway up the street before he rushed after her. He grunted and pointed at the rock sitting next to the curb.

"No, I can't go with you, Mr. Tarp. I… I don't like the thunder. I need to go home."

There was no point trying to explain to the giant. He couldn't understand. Jenny felt bad for not helping him get home, but she needed to get away from the thunder, and there was no thunder back home.

Mr. Tarp put his arm down to stop Jenny from moving further away. She climbed over his outstretched hand and kept walking up the street. The giant moved to block her again, but Jenny began running. Mr. Tarp looked like he was going to give chase, until Jenny rounded a corner and kept running. Instead, he bowed his head and slowly went back to his rock.

Chapter 7

Jenny ran and ran. She had no idea where she was. It was so dark that she could barely read the street signs, not that it mattered since she wasn't even in her own neighborhood anymore.

The only thing that scared Jenny more than thunder was being lost and alone. She was about to go up to one of the houses and start knocking on the door when a car pulled around the corner. Red and blue lights flashed as it pulled over. The door opened and a policewoman stepped out with a flashlight in her hand.

"What are you doing out here, kid?!"

Jenny started to cry. She quickly peeked over her shoulder and saw that Mr. Tarp had disappeared. When she turned back around, the policewoman was standing in front of her.

"What are you doing out here, honey? Do you live in one of these houses?"

"N-no," said Jenny through the tears. "I'm… I'm lost."

The policewoman took her hand and led her back to her car. Jenny kept looking over her shoulder, expecting to see Mr. Tarp appear, but there was nobody else around.

Once Jenny had climbed into the front seat of the car, the officer fastened her seatbelt. She went to the back of the car and pulled something out of the trunk before returning and entering her own seat.

"Here," she said, giving Jenny a large blanket. "Dry yourself off. You're going to catch something."

Jenny wiped her face with the blanket. She didn't realize how wet she'd gotten during her trip with Mr. Tarp. The rain was falling harder now.

"What's your name?" asked the officer.

"Jenny Spotter."

A look of surprise crossed the policewoman's face. She quickly checked something on the computer next to the steering wheel.

"Spotter… Spotter…" she muttered. "Do you live at 510 Monroe Avenue?"

Jenny nodded.

The officer sighed. "We were at your house earlier tonight. Something about a man wandering around outside your house?"

This time, Jenny didn't respond.

"Let's get you home," said the policewoman.

The drive home was quiet. At one point, the officer called in to the police station on her walkie-talkie to report that she had picked up a lost child. Jenny tuned in and out of the conversation; she was too busy thinking about two things: how her parents were going to react when they found out she had left the house, and what Mr. Tarp was doing now that he was all alone.

There had been no thunder since that moment before Jenny left Mr. Tarp. She was curious as to where he was now. Probably still kicking that stupid rock down the street. Jenny wondered how long before anyone else saw him. There was no way a giant could make it to Olympus Hill without being seen.

"I'm Detective Rodriguez," the policewoman said. "But you can call me Heather, if you want."

Jenny didn't say anything. She glanced at the clock on the radio. It was almost five o'clock in the morning! No wonder she was so tired.

"So what were you doing halfway across town at this hour in the rain?" asked Heather.

Jenny wasn't sure how to answer. Should she tell the truth and explain how she was helping her giant friend get back home?

"I was trying to find out where the thunder went," Jenny finally said.

Heather raised an eyebrow. "What are you talking about?"

"There hasn't been any thunder all night. I was trying to find out where it went."

The police car turned a corner. Heather waited until they reached a traffic light before she spoke again. "I'll be honest, I still don't get what you mean."

Jenny decided it was best to tell a little bit of the truth.

"My dad told me about these giants called Thunder-Kickers and how they—"

"— kick the clouds and cause thunderstorms," finished Heather with a nod. "Yeah, your dad told us. My parents told me the same thing when I was your age. 'Course, by the time I was old enough, I found out the truth."

Jenny tilted her head, much like how Mr. Tarp did. "Truth?"

"Well, I don't exactly know the entire scientific side of it, but thunder isn't caused by any giants. It's stuff like air pressure and temperature and the atmosphere. I don't know; I wasn't that good at science in school."

Jenny smirked. She knew an adult wouldn't understand. If only Heather had met Mr. Tarp. Then she'd see what *really* caused thunder.

"I hate it," Jenny said. "Thunder. It's so loud."

"Oh, I do too," said Heather. "It wakes me up when I'm trying to sleep, and with my job, I like to get as much sleep as I can."

"You mean thunder scares you too? But you're a police officer! And a grown-up!"

Heather shook her head. "I didn't say I was scared. I just hate it. There's nothing to really be scared of when it comes to thunder. It's only noise."

"But it's scary…"

"It *sounds* scary, but so do a lot of things. And it can't hurt you. Why would you be scared of something that can't hurt you, like thunder?"

Jenny paused, then shrugged.

"I don't know," said Heather quietly. "You're a kid, so it's okay to be scared. Maybe you'll grow out of it. But you can't always wait for the storm to pass. You have to face it. That's how you deal with anything that scares you."

Jenny paused again. Looking at her feet, she mumbled, "I wasn't looking for the thunder."

"Yeah, I figured as much," replied Heather. "Why would a kid go looking for thunder if she's so scared of it?"

"I was trying to help my friend get home," said Jenny, still staring at her feet. She could sense that Heather had a confused look on her face.

"What do you mean?"

"My friend wanted to go home, but he didn't know the way. I was helping him get home."

Heather stopped the car.

"Are you saying there's another kid out there in this weather? Why wasn't he with you when I stopped?"

Jenny fought back tears. "I left him because I heard thunder and I got scared. I left him all alone."

Heather took a deep breath. After a few seconds, she rubbed Jenny's shoulder.

"It's okay. Don't worry."

Jenny looked up as she felt the car turning around. Heather was driving back to where she found her.

"Let's go find your friend."

Chapter 8

Heather drove back to the street where she found Jenny. Mr. Tarp was nowhere to be found, and neither was his rock. The police car slowly made its way up and down the road as Heather and Jenny looked all around for some sign of life.

"What does your friend look like?" Heather asked as she squinted through the rain.

"Uh… he's tall."

Heather raised an eyebrow. "And?"

"Uh… really tall."

"That's not doing much for me, kid," said Heather, rolling her eyes. "Do you know what he was wearing?"

"A blue shirt and blue pants," Jenny admitted. "He's got really dark skin, but really light hair."

For a second, Jenny thought she saw Heather look at her like she was crazy. But the detective said nothing and kept her eyes focused to her side of the road.

The police car spent another couple of minutes cruising around the blocks. Jenny tried to get Heather to drive toward Olympus Hill, but she wasn't even sure if Mr. Tarp was heading in that direction. He was probably letting the rock guide his way. Who knows where he would end up?

The storm continued. It was still mostly dark out. Over the horizon, it looked like the clouds were breaking and the tiniest bit of sun was showing.

"If we want to find your friend," said Heather after a long silence, "then we'll probably need to get another squad car out here. The more eyes, the better. I'll take you home and call for backup."

"Wait," Jenny said suddenly. "I think I know where he might've gone. Can we please check there before you call?"

"Where?"

"Olympus Hill."

"The Hill?" asked Heather. "Why would he be all the way out there? It's nothing but farms and fields."

"Please, can we just go that way? I promise you can call more officers and take me home and whatever you want to do. I want to check this one last place."

Much like last time, Heather waited a few seconds before responding. She then spun the car around and headed toward the large hill in the distance. Jenny prayed that Mr. Tarp's rock would've taken him in that direction.

The rain pounded against the police car's windows. The storm had gotten so strong all of a sudden, but it was just rain, no lightning or thunder in sight.

"This storm is out of control," said Heather, scrunching her eyes to see out her window.

"No thunder," whispered Jenny.

"Yeah, true. No lightning either. But I guess that's a good thing, though, right?"

The police car zoomed up the road slowly. Jenny kept her eyes wide open in case she spotted something huge shuffling along with a rock at its feet. Some of the houses had their lights on already. Time was running out. They needed to find Mr. Tarp and get Jenny back home soon.

Just as Jenny felt her hope starting to disappear, Heather stomped on the brake pedal, bringing her car to a stop. Jenny felt her heart drop into her stomach. A rock rolled across the street in front of them. Heather and Jenny turned their heads at the same time and saw a familiar-looking giant making his way through the rain.

Heather's jaw dropped. "What in the world—"

"Mr. Tarp!" yelled Jenny.

The giant couldn't hear her through the window or over the rain. He walked down the street and kicked the stone, as he had been, but he was going the wrong way. Olympus Hill was in the opposite direction.

"I need to call back up now," said Heather, reaching for her walkie-talkie. Jenny grabbed her arm.

"No, you don't need to call anyone. That's my friend!"

"Your friend?! That's not a friend, kid. That's an over-grown gorilla that must've escaped from the zoo or something!"

Heather reached for the walkie again, but before she could say anything, Jenny had jumped out of her car and was running down the street after the giant.

"Mr. Tarp!" screamed Jenny, waving her arms in the air.

The giant still couldn't hear her over the rain. Jenny took a deep breath and got ready to scream again, when a lightning bolt zapped across the sky, quickly followed by a tremendous roar of thunder.

It was possibly the loudest thunderstrike Jenny had ever heard in her life. It was so loud, she felt the entire world shake beneath her feet. Once again, she found herself unable to move a muscle. She stood there, hypnotized by the rumbling.

"Jenny!" Heather appeared behind her and grabbed her arm. "Get back in my car, now! I can't tell you how dangerous it is to be out here!"

When Jenny didn't respond, Heather huffed and began dragging her back to the car. With each passing second, Mr. Tarp was moving further and further away from Olympus Hill, which meant further and further away from getting home. Jenny wanted to help, but she couldn't. Thunder cracked overhead, making her whimper in fright.

But then something came over her. She remembered what Heather had said earlier. *You have to face it. That's how you deal with anything that scares you.*

Heather was right; Jenny couldn't clam up every time there was a storm and wait for it to pass. It was time for her to do something, especially now, or else Mr. Tarp would never get home.

The rain had made Jenny's arm slippery, allowing her to wriggle out of Heather's grasp.

"Hey!" yelled the detective.

Jenny darted around the corner of the block and followed Mr. Tarp. His kicks weren't as powerful as they were earlier, so he and the rock hadn't traveled as far. Now, every time he kicked the rock, it only went two or three houses down.

Thunder struck again. That was three times in less than ten minutes, the most thunder there had been all night. Jenny could feel her chest tighten and her legs get stiff when she heard that rumble in the sky above, but this time, she managed to push through it. She was not going to let her fear stop her from helping her new friend get home.

Jenny reached the rock and stood in front of it with her arms wide open. Mr. Tarp stopped and stared at her, doing that familiar head-tilt that showed that he was confused. Jenny waved her arms to signal him to go the other direction, toward the big hill looming over the town. Again, the giant didn't seem to notice. Instead, he stepped around Jenny and kicked the rock in his original direction.

More thunder came. This time, Jenny didn't even react to it because she was too frustrated with Mr. Tarp's stubbornness. That stupid giant was too busy with his stupid rock. If she were strong enough, Jenny would've kicked the rock toward Olympus Hill and hoped the giant would follow.

Heather's car appeared around the corner and pulled up to Jenny.

"You are absolutely crazy, you know that?!" yelled the detective. "Now get in my car so I can take you home!"

Jenny didn't listen. An idea was forming in her head. The rock was too heavy for her to carry to the Hill, and she'd need something that could move faster than Mr. Tarp; something like a car…

"Follow him!" Jenny said as she jumped into the police car.

Heather looked at her like she had five heads.

"Excuse me?! I'm not following that… thing. I'm taking you home now and calling the station for a backup unit. I might even call animal control while I'm at it."

"No, please, you need to listen. He's a Thunder-Kicker! He needs to get back to his home in the sky, but the only way he can do that is if he jumps off a really high place, like Olympus Hill. We need to lead him that way!"

Heather's hands rested on the steering wheel. It looked like she was struggling between listening to what Jenny was saying, and completely ignoring her and taking the little girl straight home. Heather stared at Mr. Tarp as he kicked the stone two more times.

"Let me guess, you want to use that rock as bait?"

Jenny shrugged. "You got a better idea?"

This was almost too much for Heather to handle. She rubbed her hands into her eyes, as if making sure she really was seeing a giant in front of her. Then, she gave one of her usual loud sighs, and took off down the street.

"This is probably the weirdest thing I've ever done, but I guess we gotta do something. Let's help this guy get home."

Chapter 9

"How are we going to get that rock from him?" asked Heather. "I'm not planning on getting in the way of those feet."

"Let me distract him. You open up your trunk and throw it in there," said Jenny.

"This is *definitely* the weirdest thing I've ever done," Heather said quietly.

The car pulled up a few yards ahead of the giant. Jenny jumped out and ran up to Mr. Tarp, waving her arms and doing a little dance to get his attention. She was so caught up in her moves that she didn't hear the two thunderclaps that happened right after each other. Mr. Tarp seemed to be distracted by the little dancing girl as well and didn't even notice Heather picking up his rock and carrying it to her trunk.

"Come on, Mr. Tarp!" yelled Jenny. "Follow me!"

The little girl ran back toward the police car. Mr. Tarp didn't follow at first. He looked at his feet, then behind him to see where his beloved rock went. When he saw it sitting in the back of the car, he let out a groan that was loud enough to be heard over the rain.

"UHHHHHHHHHHHH!"

Jenny jumped into the car and fastened her seatbelt. Heather didn't wait for her to say anything before she stomped on the gas pedal, steering the car past the giant's feet and up the road toward Olympus Hill.

Behind them, the giant howled in the storm. Jenny looked back and saw him begin to chase after the car. He may have had long legs, but luckily, he wasn't fast enough to catch up to them.

"Don't go too fast!" warned Jenny. "We don't want to lose him."

"Thanks for the tip!" said Heather with a smirk. "It's not every day I'm trying to get a giant to follow my car."

Olympus Hill was coming up fast. One more stoplight and the car would start going uphill. The light turned red as the car reached it, but Heather simply pressed her foot down harder, sending them flying up the street. Jenny watched as Mr. Tarp ran through the red light without looking both ways. His parents probably wouldn't be happy about that.

The thunder seemed to be happening more often now that they were on Olympus Hill. Jenny felt her heart skip a beat every time the lightning struck, warning her of the incoming crash of thunder. But she wasn't scared like she used to be. Now, the thunder hardly bothered her more than the rain did.

The tires squealed as they struggled to pull the police car up the hill. Mr. Tarp was gaining on them fast.

"Go faster!" demanded Jenny.

"I can't!" replied Heather. "This hill is terrible in the rain and snow."

Jenny saw Mr. Tarp coming up quickly. The way he was moving, it seemed like he was getting ready…

… to launch a mighty kick.

"Go! Go! Go!" said Jenny.

Everything moved in slow motion. Heather kept pressing the gas pedal while Jenny urged her to go.

Mr. Tarp was only ten steps away now.

Then five steps.

Then three, two, one…

With a loud yell, Heather stomped the gas pedal as hard as she could, and the police car jumped forward like a rabbit and sped up the hill. A split-second later, Mr. Tarp's foot swung through the air, barely missing his target. The giant groaned and chased after the car.

Within minutes, the police car came to a stop at the very top of Olympus Hill. It was at that same moment that it stopped raining. The dark storm clouds still loomed overhead, but the distant sun was quickly making its way over the horizon, lighting up the town.

"It's beautiful," said Jenny, getting out of the car.

Heather pulled the rock out of the trunk of her car and placed it on the ground several yards away. Seconds later, the sounds of Mr. Tarp's groans made their way to the top of the hill. Jenny stood there with a big smile as the giant came into view.

Mr. Tarp came to a sudden stop once he saw his precious rock on the ground. He gave a toothy grin to Jenny and Heather (who was standing in front of the little girl with her hand on her nightstick).

"Now what?" asked the detective.

Mr. Tarp seemed just as confused. He didn't want to kick his rock anymore. He merely stood there and scratched his head.

"Now you need to jump, Mr. Tarp!" said Jenny.

The giant tilted his head.

"Jump!" Jenny hopped. She nodded at Heather. "You too. Maybe he'll get the idea?"

Heather sighed and began jumping (though not as high as Jenny was). The two of them jumped over and over while yelling at the giant to do the same. Mr. Tarp watched them for several seconds before he began to hop as well. He gave a few small leaps at first, hardly high enough to make it over Jenny, but after a few tries, his jumps got higher. Soon, he was jumping higher than a house.

"Keep going!" Jenny said, hopping higher and higher with Heather.

Finally, Mr. Tarp bent his knees down as low as he could go, and launched himself high into the air, but he didn't come back down. Instead, he kept going higher and higher, soaring into the air like a bird, until he became a little black dot in the sky. Jenny and Heather watched the dot keep getting smaller until it poked through a cloud and disappeared.

Chapter 10

The storm clouds grew lighter as Heather drove

Jenny home. Every now and then, there was a flash of

lightning, followed by the thunder. Jenny pressed her face

up against the car window so she could watch. It was

awesome seeing the lightning bolt zigzag through the sky

and then fade away, leaving behind its imprint on the

clouds.

"I never thought about how beautiful thunderstorms

can be," Jenny said. "I was always too scared to notice

before."

Heather gave a small smile and nodded, but she didn't say anything as she continued driving.

It was early morning when they arrived at Jenny's house. When they pulled up, Jenny squinted to see if she could spot her family in the windows. Nothing. Maybe they were still asleep. If they were, they were about to wake up to quite a surprise.

"I don't know what I'm going to tell my parents when they find out I've been out all night," said Jenny, frowning. "I'm going to be grounded for the rest of my life."

"Only if you tell them," said Heather.

Jenny looked at the detective. "Aren't you going to tell them that you found me in the middle of the night?"

"I should," admitted Heather. "I should tell them about everything that happened last night. But even *I* don't believe it."

After the police car parked in front of the house. Heather and Jenny got out and made their way to the door. Taking a deep breath, Jenny reached out to knock, but Heather grabbed her hand.

"Hang on." She looked through the windows. "I think everyone's asleep."

"Yeah, probably because it's Saturday. My mom and dad always sleep late on the weekend, unless my little brother wakes them up."

Heather bit her lip. "Do you have a key to get in?"

Jenny pulled a key from her pocket. Heather gave a half-smile. She looked around, like she was making sure the coast was clear. When she saw nobody in the area, she bent down and whispered to the little girl.

"I could get fired for this. I shouldn't even *think* of doing something like this, but I don't want to see you get in trouble after the night we've been through."

The two stared at each other for a moment, during which Heather glanced over her shoulder again.

"I want you to quietly go inside and head right to bed. Don't tell your parents anything about what happened tonight. This will stay between you and me. Do you understand?"

For a moment, Jenny felt happy that she may not get in trouble after all. But she was upset that she was being told to keep tonight a secret.

"But we helped Mr. Tarp get home. Thunder-Kickers are real! Why can't we tell anyone?"

"Shhh," said Heather softly. "I know you want to tell the world all about this. Trust me, I would too. But some things are better left as secrets. What we did for Mr. Tarp is one of those things. We can't ever tell anybody about what happened, unless you want me to get fired and for you to never leave your room ever again."

This only made Jenny feel worse. She looked down at her feet. At this point, she didn't care about getting in trouble. All she wanted to do was tell her parents how Thunder-Kickers are real and how she helped her new friend get home and how she wasn't afraid of thunder anymore. But a small part of her knew that Heather was right. What happened last night had to be their secret forever.

"Fine," mumbled Jenny. "I won't tell anyone."

"Hey," said Heather, smiling and lifting Jenny's chin up. "You should be proud. Most people will never get to do what you did."

"Help a giant get home?" asked Jenny.

Heather chuckled. "Well, yeah. But also facing their fears like you did. You were really brave, braver than I ever was at your age. You're a rockstar."

Jenny threw herself into Heather's arms for a big hug.

"Be safe," said Heather, "and don't ever go out at night alone ever again!" said Heather, wagging her finger. She stood up and walked back to her car. Jenny slowly opened the door, taking care not to make any noise. She gave one last look back at Heather, who was watching from her car, waved, and then went inside.

As quietly as she had the night before, Jenny made her way up to her room. She had left her raincoat and boots by the backdoor and used paper towels to wipe up any footprints along the way. Her parents would never know of her nighttime adventure.

The clock read 6:45 when she finally crawled into bed. She didn't realize how tired she was until she pulled the warm covers over her. It was like she hadn't slept in years. Jenny turned over and closed her eyes, falling asleep almost instantly.

A loud crash of thunder woke Jenny up hours later. She sat up, rubbed her eyes a little, and looked out the window. The storm was back again, and the rain loudly pounded against her windows. A few seconds passed before thunder struck again, this time louder than before.

The bedroom door opened. Jenny's mom poked her head in.

"Oh, I knew the thunder would wake you up, honey. Are you okay? Did you want to come sit with me in my office?"

"No, I think I'm fine," Jenny said with a tired smile.

Mom raised an eyebrow.

"You sure? We know how you get during thunderstorms. Did you want one of us to stay in here with you until the storm passes? It could go on for a while."

At that moment, thunder cracked outside, the loudest one yet. Mom glanced at Jenny, who gave one of the widest yawns ever.

"Mom, I'm okay," said Jenny, lying back down. "The thunder doesn't scare me anymore." She paused. "But if you or Dad are scared, you guys can come watch TV with me until the storm is done."

Jenny's mom smiled at her and closed the door, leaving her at peace. Jenny turned on her side so she could watch the storm while she fell back asleep. As thunder struck once more, she wondered if Mr. Tarp was up there right now, kicking the clouds above her house.

The End